To Sean
– Hyewon Yum

For Helen, Zoë, and Isaac—my happiness
– Bruce Handy

The Happiness
of a Dog with
a Ball in Its Mouth

Bruce Handy & Hyewon Yum

Enchanted Lion Books
NEW YORK

The slowness of two eyes opening.

The happiness of a new day.

The patience of a dog at the door.

The happiness of a dog with a ball in its mouth.

The nervousness of a beginning.

The happiness of a middle.

The indignity of a cut.

The happiness of a scab.

The stillness of a perch.

The happiness of flight.

The worry of looking.

The frustration of hearing ...

The happiness of finding.

The happiness of saying ...

NO!

(Once in a while.)

The divide of
mine.

The happiness of **ours**.

The distance of a journey.

The happiness of getting there.

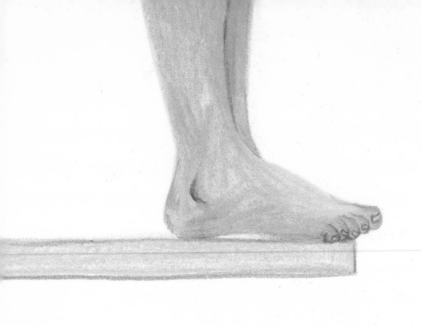

The fear of leaping.

The happiness of having leapt.

The effort of holding in.

The happiness of letting go.

The self-sufficiency of a cat in the morning.

The happiness of a cat in the afternoon.

The difficulty of a choice.

The happiness of a decision.
(Or two.)

The boredom of nothing to do.

The happiness of nothing to do.

The ache of a loss.

The happiness of a memory.
(And the sadness, too.)

The reluctance of getting out.

The happiness of a change.

The sameness of sameness.

The happiness of getting in.

The aloneness of a room.

The happiness of a home.

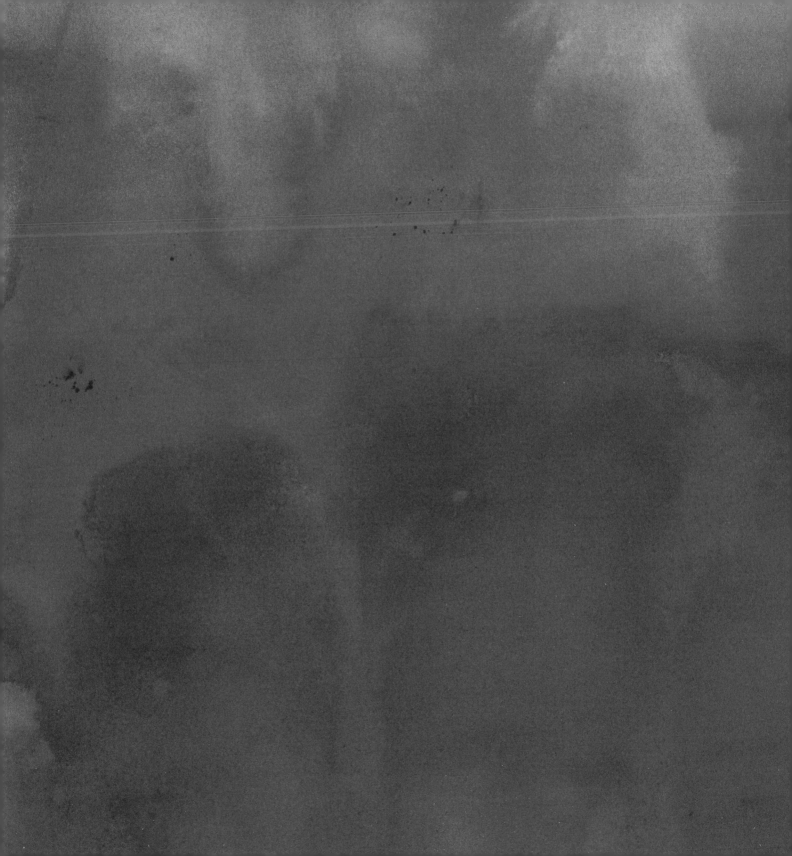

The mystery of sleep.

The happiness of another new day.

www.enchantedlion.com

First edition published in 2021 by Enchanted Lion Books
248 Creamer Street, Studio 4, Brooklyn, NY 11231
Text copyright © 2021 by Bruce Handy
Illustrations copyright © 2021 by Hyewon Yum
Book design by Lawrence Kim
A CIP is on record with the Library of Congress
ISBN 978-1-59270-351-7
Printed in Italy by Societa Editoriale Grafiche AZ
First Printing